First published by Parragon in 2012
Parragon
Chartist House
15–17 Trim Street
Bath BA1 1HA, UK
www.parragon.com

Edited by: Gemma Louise Lowe
Designed by: Jim Willmott
Production by: Jack Aylward

ISBN 978-1-78186-034-2

Printed in China

DISNEY·PIXAR
MONSTERS, INC.

Bath · New York · Singapore · Hong Kong · Cologne · Delhi
Melbourne · Amsterdam · Johannesburg · Shenzhen

A teacher at Monsters, Incorporated was repeating the rules to her pupils: Never scream. And NEVER leave a child's cupboard door open. Why?

"It could let in a child!" bellowed Mr Waternoose, the boss of Monsters, Inc.

The Scarers-in-Training gasped. They knew that children's screams powered Monstropolis. But letting a child into the world of monsters would be deadly to everyone!

Meanwhile, across town, James P. Sullivan was training. His assistant (and best friend), Mike Wazowski, was coaching him. Sulley was a professional Scarer and he needed to keep in top shape.

"Feel the burn," Mike urged. "You call yourself a monster?!"

At Monsters, Inc., Sulley was famous for collecting the most screams.

That was important because the city was having an energy shortage. Human kids were getting harder to scare, and Monstropolis needed all the screams it could get.

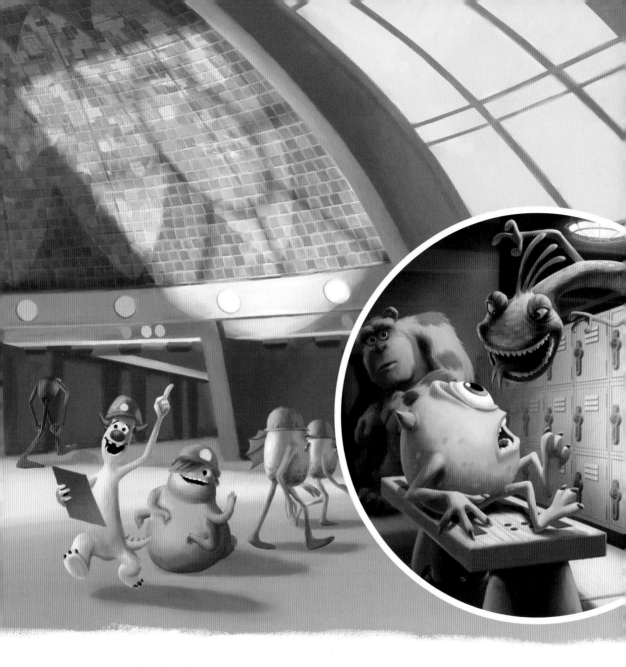

In the locker room, a monster named Randall popped out at Mike.

"AHHH!" Mike shrieked.

Randall was creepy and mean ... and very jealous of Sulley. Randall would do anything to be the top Scarer.

It was time for the workday to begin. All the Scarers walked out onto the Scare Floor – these were the best scream collectors in the business.

As the Scarers prepared for work, a conveyor belt dropped a door at each station. Each Scarer would walk through their door – into the room of a sleeping child.

Hopefully, the child would let out a good scream!

When work was finished, Mike rushed to meet his girlfriend, Celia, for a date. But the company's file clerk, Roz, blocked Mike's way.

"I'm sure you filed your paperwork," she rasped.

Mike had forgotten! Luckily, Sulley offered to help.

When Sulley got back to the Scare Floor, he noticed that someone had left a door behind. He peeked through the door, but saw no one. So he closed the door. Then he saw ... A CHILD!

"AAAAH!" he screamed.

Mike and Celia were enjoying a romantic date. Suddenly, Mike spotted Sulley outside of the window.

Sulley quickly explained about the child. Mike was horrified ... especially when Sulley showed him the girl!

When the CDA (Child Detection Agency) arrived, Mike and Sulley hid the girl in a box and ran. They were in big trouble!

Back at home, Sulley and Mike tried not to let the child touch them.

Then Mike accidentally fell and the little girl started to giggle. Strangely, her laughter made the lights burn brighter!

When Sulley put the child to bed, she was afraid that Randall was in the cupboard. So Sulley stayed until she fell asleep.

"This might sound crazy," Sulley told Mike later, "but I don't think that kid is dangerous."

The next morning, Mike and Sulley disguised the girl and took her to work. They needed to put her back in her door.

In the locker room, Sulley and the child played hide-and-seek. "Boo!" she said playfully.

Sulley was starting to really like her. But then they overheard Randall tell his assistant that he planned to 'take care of the kid'.

Sulley needed to get the little girl home quickly!

Mike tried to find the right door, but he made a mistake. "This isn't Boo's door," Sulley exclaimed.

"Boo?!" Mike couldn't believe Sulley had named the child. And Boo had a nickname for Sulley, too: 'Kitty'.

Meanwhile, Boo wandered off!

Mike and Sulley split up to find Boo, and Randall cornered Mike. The nasty monster knew all about Boo. He told Mike to bring her to the Scare Floor. He said he'd have her door ready....

After they found Boo, Mike and Sulley took her to the Scare Floor, where a door was waiting. But Sulley was still worried.

To prove the open door was safe, Mike went right through – and was grabbed by Randall!

Staying hidden, Sulley and Boo followed the mean monster and discovered that he had invented a cruel new machine. It captured screams from kids – and he was about to try it out on Mike!

Sulley rescued Mike just in time and they raced towards the training room. He needed to warn the boss, Mr Waternoose, about Randall.

In the training room, Boo accidentally saw Sulley looking scary. Sulley felt awful. For the first time, he realized how mean it was to scare a child.

Mr Waternoose promised to fix everything, but he was really working with Randall!

Mr Waternoose pushed Sulley and Mike through a door into the human world. They were banished to the Himalayan mountains!

Sulley had to get back and help Boo! He found a wardrobe door in a Himalayan village that led him home.

Then he rushed to Randall's secret lab and destroyed the new machine.

As Sulley raced away with Boo, Mike arrived to help. Celia didn't understand what was happening, so Mike quickly tried to explain!

Mike and Sulley climbed onto the machine that carried doors to the Scare Floor. The power wasn't on, but Mike had an idea. He made a funny face. When Boo laughed, the doors began to move!

But to send Boo home, they needed to find her door.

Suddenly, Randall grabbed Boo, but she fought back!

"She's not scared of you anymore," Sulley told Randall.

Working together, they beat Randall once and for all.

But Sulley, Mike and Boo weren't safe yet. Now Mr Waternoose and the CDA were controlling the doors.

While Mike distracted the CDA, Sulley escaped with Boo. Unfortunately, Mr Waternoose saw everything.

"Give me the child!" he yelled, running after Sulley.

But luckily, Mike recorded Mr Waternoose yelling, "I'll kidnap a thousand children before I let this company die!" Now all of Monstropolis knew that he had planned to steal children. He was arrested by the head of the CDA – who turned out to be Roz!

It was time for Boo to go home. Sulley followed her into her room and tucked her into bed.

Sadly, Sulley returned to Monstropolis. Roz ordered the CDA to shred Boo's door, so it couldn't be used for scaring anymore.

After that, Sulley became president of Monsters, Inc. And the Scare Floor became a Laugh Floor! Sulley and Mike had discovered that laughter produced more power than screams.

Monstropolis was saved.

Sulley still missed Boo, though. He had kept a tiny sliver of her door.

Before long, however, Mike surprised his pal. He'd put Boo's door back together! It was missing just one little piece. Sulley inserted the piece, opened the door and saw....

"Boo?" Sulley whispered.

"Kitty!" an excited voice replied.

The two friends were reunited at last.